GARMANN'S SUMMER

STIAN HOLE is an acclaimed Norwegian author and artist. His children's books include *Anna's Heaven* and *Night Guard* (both Eerdmans), and he has also created book covers for readers of \all ages. One summer evening, Stian saw a familiar fear in his oldest son's eyes: he was afraid of starting school. Soon Stian began writing the story that became *Garmann's Summer*.

DON BARTLETT has translated numerous books by Scandinavian authors, including crime novels by Jo Nesbø and picture books like *Anna's Heaven*, *Samira and the Skeletons*, and *John Jensen Feels Different* (all Eerdmans). In 2016, he was awarded the Royal Norwegian Order of Merit in rank of Knight, Class I, for his work as a translator of Norwegian literature. Don lives in Norfolk, England.

FOR ODD-OLAV

Originally published in Norway in 2006 under the title *Garmanns Sommer* by J.W. Cappelens Forlag

TEXT, COVER, ILLUSTRATIONS, AND BOOK DESIGN © 2006 Stian Hole
©2006 Cappelen
Translation © 2008 Don Bartlett

First English edition 2008
Paperback printing 2024

Published in the United States of America
by Eerdmans Books for Young Readers,
an imprint of Wm. B. Eerdmans Publishing Co.
Grand Rapids, Michigan

www.eerdmans.com/youngreaders

Published with support from the Norwegian Cultural Fund

Manufactured in China

32 31 30 29 28 27 26 25 24   1 2 3 4 5 6 7 8 9

ISBN 978-0-8028-5628-9

A catalog record of the hardcover edition is available from the Library of Congress.

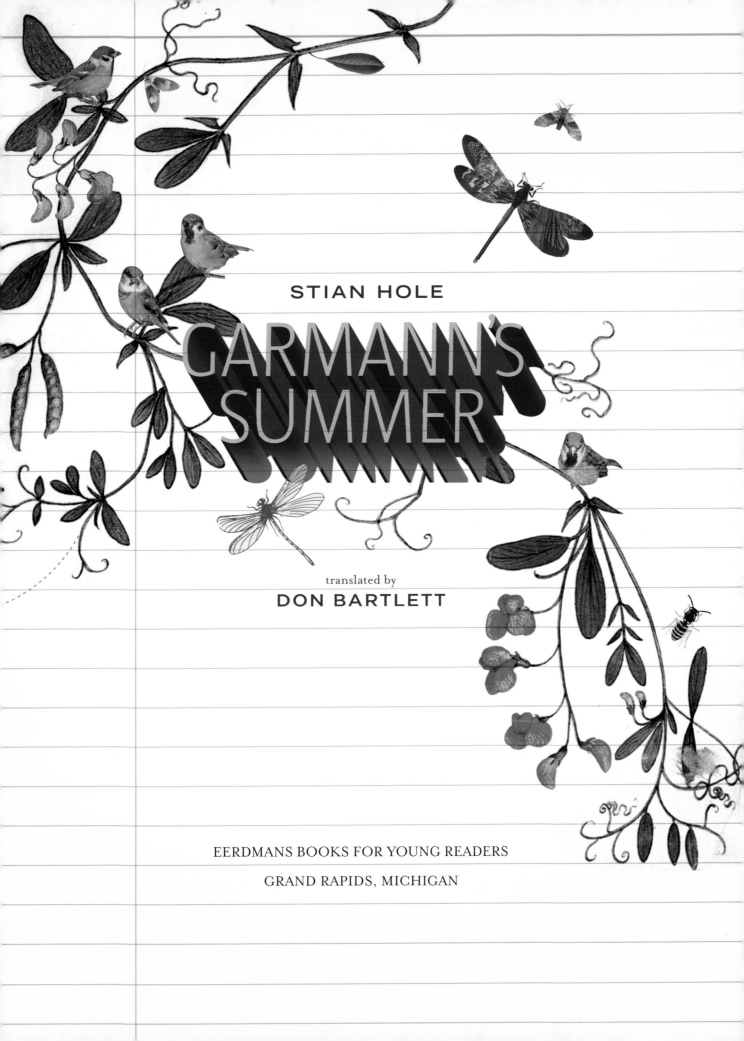

STIAN HOLE

GARMANN'S SUMMER

translated by
DON BARTLETT

EERDMANS BOOKS FOR YOUNG READERS

GRAND RAPIDS, MICHIGAN

Garmann's summer will soon be over. The grasshoppers are singing, and the three old aunts are coming to stay. Garmann closes his eyes and thinks of black slugs, itchy mosquito bites, and starting school.

He opens his eyes again and looks at the apple tree. The branches are like crooked fingers pointing to the sky. Soon it will be autumn.

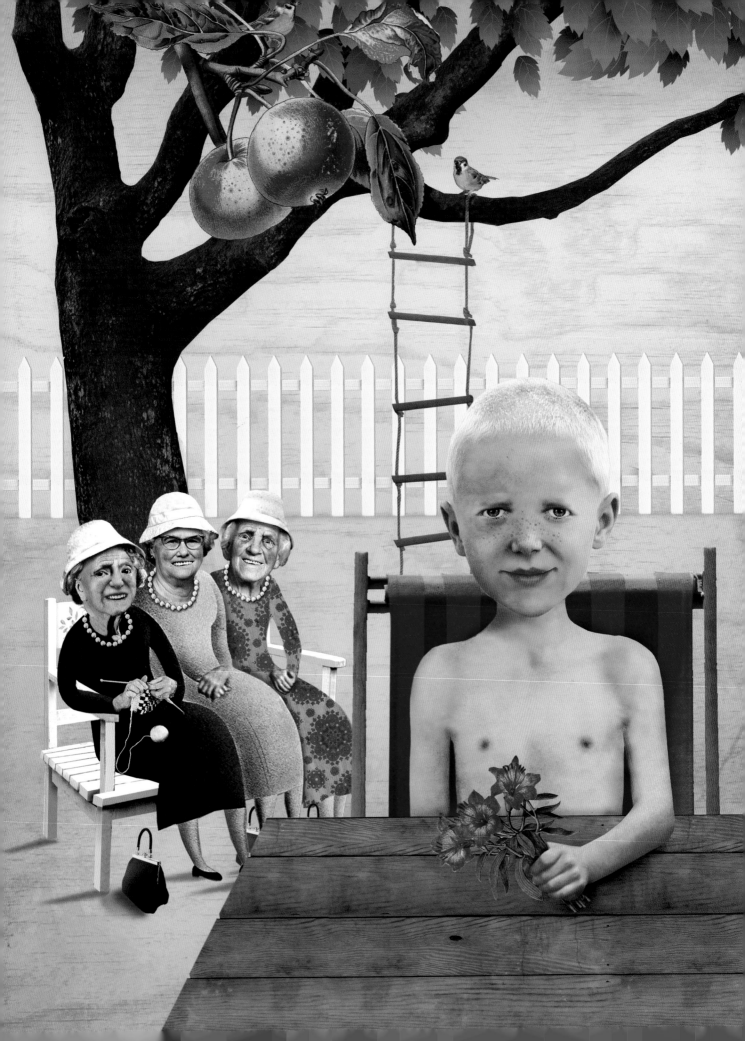

Every year the aunts come for a few days,
bringing rheumatism, hernias, and almond
tart. They arrive by boat from another time,
always with a package for Garmann.

Garmann is almost as tall as the aunts, even
though he is only six years old. Every summer the
aunts shrink a bit in the sun, thinks Garmann.
Soon they won't be able to see over the grass.

A ladybug flies in on the wind and lands on Garmann. It has six black spots on its back. Daddy says ladybugs bring luck. Garmann makes three quick wishes before he hugs the aunts. They feel soft and pillowy against his cheek.

"You are so thin and pale," the aunts say with a smile.

"Thank you. You too," Garmann says with a bow.

Before he has undone the paper, Garmann knows what is in their soft package: a knitted hat with a pom-pom on top. Not a black hat with a Batman patch, as he wanted. Garmann gets the same present every single year. Now he has six hats with pom-poms. The same number as the spots on the ladybug.

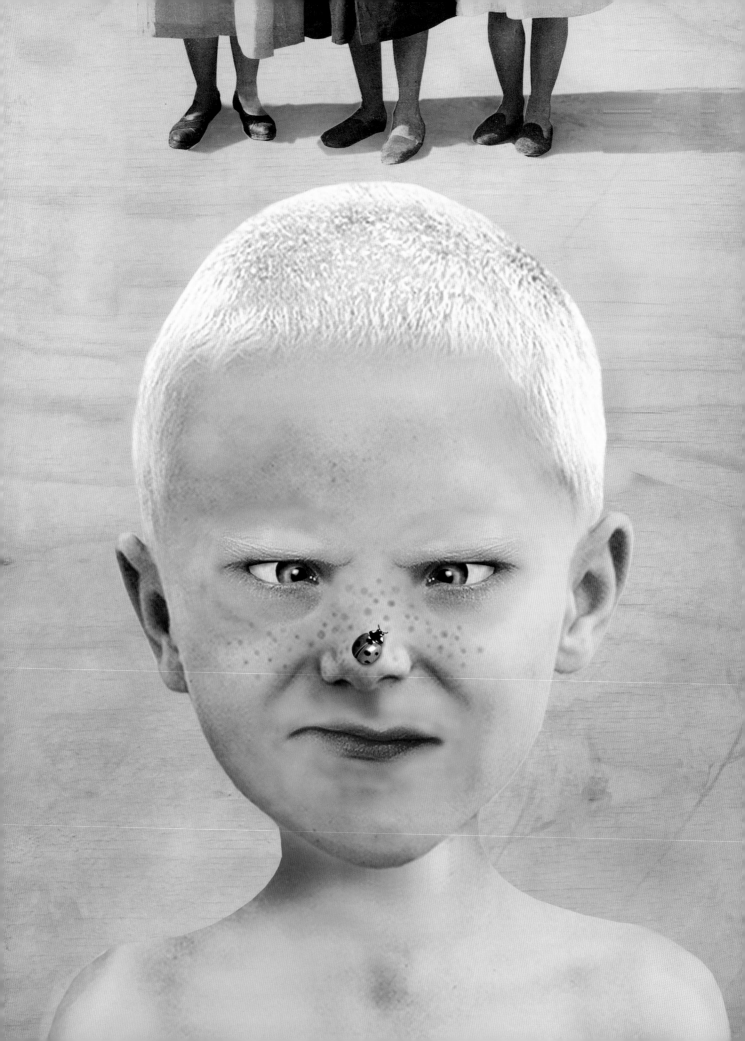

"**W**hat are you going to be when you grow up?"
Auntie Augusta whispers to Garmann, putting
a dollar bill in his hand so that the others
don't see. "A fireman or football player?"

"A fire eater," Garmann answers, putting
the money in his pocket.

"How do you feel about starting school?
Do you have butterflies in your tummy?" Auntie
Borghild asks.

"I'm scared," Garmann answers,
wondering how butterflies get into your stomach.

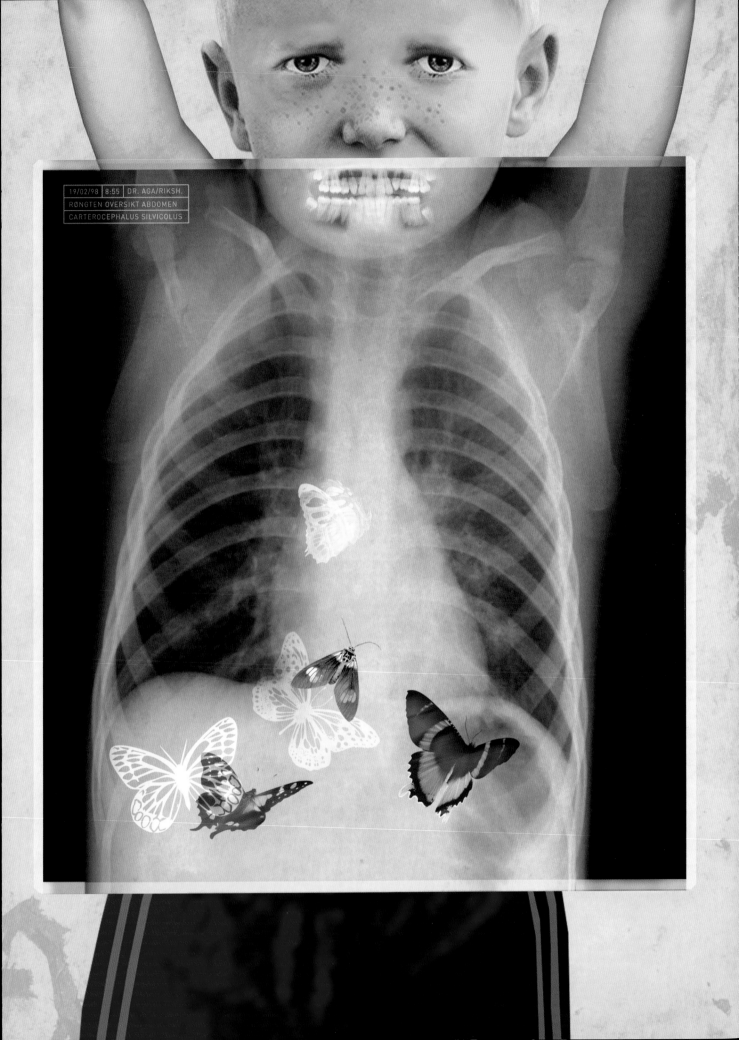

19/02/98 | 8:55 | DR. AGA/RIKSH.
RØNGTEN OVERSIKT ABDOMEN
CARTEROCEPHALUS SILVICOLUS

Auntie Ruth furrows her brow. "I'm scared too," she whispers. "Soon I will have to use a walker with wheels."

"You can borrow my skateboard," Garmann answers, imagining Auntie Ruth skating along the pavement at full speed! Auntie Ruth laughs.

$\mathcal{G}$armann climbs up the plum tree and listens to the aunts praising the brightly colored garden. They all talk at the same time, clap their hands, and flit from plant to plant like bees.

"You certainly have a green thumb!" they say to Garmann's mother.

Daddy says, "And you have roses in your cheeks, too."

Grown-ups speak in such a strange way, thinks Garmann. Listening to his aunts, he realizes that the flowers have the same names as old ladies — Gladiola, Dahlia, Chrysanthemum, Marigold, and Petunia.

I can read.
I can ride my bicycle
I have lost both
my front teeth,
I am starting first grade

I like rhubarb
Mama likes rhubarb
Daddy likes rhubarb
We all like
brabuhr,

that is rhubarb
spelled
backwards,

Not one of Garmann's teeth is loose yet, and school begins tomorrow. Now it's urgent!

Every evening, all summer, Garmann has been feeling his teeth in front of the mirror. The neighbor girls, Hannah and Johanna, have both lost their two front teeth. They are going to start first grade, too.

The twins can do everything Garmann doesn't dare to do: bicycle, walk tightrope on the fence, and hold their heads under water. And they can already read, and they can spell "rhubarb" — backwards and forwards. Garmann feels his front teeth again, but no matter how hard he presses, they will not budge.

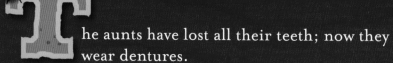he aunts have lost all their teeth; now they wear dentures.

After lunch, the aunts take a snooze in the backyard. Garmann sneaks over for a peek at their teeth. Auntie Ruth and Auntie Augusta have put their dentures in a glass of water. But Auntie Borghild has just loosened hers. Every time she breathes out, her teeth slide back and forth.

untie Borghild has lots of wrinkles and long, white hairs on her chin. The wrinkles remind Garmann of rings on a tree. He traces a vein on the thick white skin of her hand with his fingers.

Blind people use their fingers to see, Garmann thinks, and closes his eyes. Auntie's skin feels like paper.

Suddenly, she wakes with a start and adjusts her dentures.

Garmann asks, "Were you ever a child?"

Auntie Borghild thinks for a while. A dragonfly hovers in the air. Then she smiles and speaks. "Yes, a hundred and fifty years ago," she says, and laughs so hard she shakes.

"Are you going to die soon?" Garmann asks. Auntie Borghild looks up at the branches of the apple tree. "Yes, it probably won't be long now." She straightens her dress. "Then I'll put on my lipstick and my best dress and travel in the great starry wagon in the sky until I come to a large gate. I'll go through the gate and wander into a garden as beautiful as yours, just a bit bigger!"

"Are you scared?" Garmann asks.

Auntie Borghild nods slowly. She takes a hairbrush from her bag and runs it through her silver-grey hair, which glistens in the sun. "Yes, Garmann, I'm scared of leaving you. But the big garden could be exciting."

Auntie Ruth is the next to wake.

"What are you scared of?" Garmann asks.

"The long winter," Auntie Ruth answers. "All old ladies are scared of winter — the cold, dark nights and snowplows and slippery pavement and shoveling snow. And trudging through the snow in heavy boots with a walker."

Strange that anyone could be scared of the winter, thinks Garmann, imagining the snowmen he is going to build and sledding in the park and hot chocolate with marshmallows.

Auntie Augusta isn't scared of anything. She is a bit forgetful and doesn't remember what it is like to be scared. "I'm so looking forward to the almond tart," she says when Garmann asks.

If you can't remember anything, you have nothing to be scared of, Garmann thinks.

"Are you scared of anything?" Daddy and Garmann are sitting on the doorstep drinking juice. Daddy doesn't seem to hear the question.

Almost every evening Daddy plays the violin in the orchestra pit at the theater. Sometimes Garmann is allowed to go too, but he can't see his dad in the dark, even though Daddy sits on a cushion. If Garmann stares hard, now and then he can catch the violin bow sticking up over the edge.

Tomorrow Daddy is going on tour with the orchestra. Garmann has seen the black suit and the violin case ready in the hall.

"I'm scared of leaving you and Mama," Daddy says finally. "And I always get scared before a concert. What if I play too fast?" He takes a deep breath. "I think everyone is scared of something."

"Even Hannah and Johanna?"

"Even Hannah and Johanna," Daddy says. Then he goes to the attic to practice.

Tomorrow Mama will take Garmann to school. She already bought him a new lunchbox and a new backpack. She will help him tie his shoelaces and button his shirt. When they get to the main road, they will look both ways before Garmann crosses. Mama and Garmann have been practicing that all summer.

Smallville

Surrounding the garden is a hedge with secret passages inside. Hundreds of tiny sparrows live in there. If Garmann sits absolutely still, they will come out. He creeps in and gives a few crumbs to the birds, who twitter and warble with delight.

There is a dead sparrow on the ground. Garmann picks it up in his hand and strokes it gently. The grey feathers at the back of its neck are still soft. He puts the bird in a big, empty matchbox and buries it in the ground. Then he makes a cross with two sticks and places it on top.

Garmann hears the aunts' voices, laughter, and the clink of coffee cups in the garden. When you die, you travel in the great starry wagon in the sky, thinks Garmann, but first of all you have to be buried.

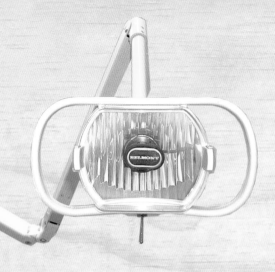

Mama clears the table while the aunts play checkers.

"Are you scared of anything, Mama?" Garmann whispers from inside the hedge.

Mama looks around. Then she crouches down on the grass and speaks very softly to the hedge. "I'm scared of Garmann crossing the main road on his way to school. The cars go so fast. I hope he will be careful."

She gets to her feet and brushes the grass off her knees. Then, on her way to the house with the cups, she stops and goes back to the hedge. She whispers, "I'm also scared to go to the dentist on Tuesday."

That reminds Garmann of something. He presses every one of his teeth as hard as he can.

The aunts are leaving. They have all the time in the world, but no time to lose.

The three old ladies fill their bags with homemade jam and flowers and magazines and say, "What a wonderful show the summer put on this year!"

Garmann wishes summer had only just started. Mama puts her red dress back in the attic.

Garmann is allowed to go down to the bay and watch the boats. Three deep blasts of the ship's horn and the aunts leave the town behind them. He watches them getting smaller and smaller. Soon they will be traveling into heaven.

They wave to Garmann until the boat is a dot merging into the clouds.

On the very last evening of summer, Garmann checks his school bag once again. He organizes his pencil case. One soccer ball eraser, eight colored pencils, a new pencil sharpener, a broken ruler, and two sharp pencils. He puts everything in the case and makes sure the zipper runs smoothly.

The wasps on the windowsill are dozy. His sixth summer went much too fast, Garmann thinks. As he buckles his backpack, he can feel a cool breeze. From the corner of his eye he sees the first leaf falling from the apple tree. Before going to bed he checks his teeth one last time to see if any are loose.

Thirteen hours to go before school starts. And Garmann is scared.